THIS BLOOMSBURY BOOK

BELONGS TO

....

For Ninesh and Mia — BE
For Ronda — DA

This edition published for Igloo Books Ltd in 2007

First published in Great Britain in 2000 by Bloomsbury Publishing Plc
38 Soho Square, London W1V 5DF

A CIP catalogue record for this book is available from the British Library.
ISBN 0 7475 5018 2 (paperback)
ISBN 0 7475 4465 4 (hardback)

Designed by Dawn Apperley

Printed and bound by South China Printing Co.

3 5 7 9 10 8 6 4 2

My Cat Charlie

Becky Edwards and David Armitage

Charlie is my cat. He's big and black and soft and he's my best friend. Every day he watches from the window, waiting for me to come home from school.

When I run through the door, he looks at me with his huge green eyes, wiggles his long whiskers and purrs loudly.

We are always happy to see each other.

Whenever we can, we play together in the garden. Charlie loves to be outside.

Sometimes we sit in the damp grass by our little pond and watch the sparkly goldfish flashing by.

Charlie swishes his tail whenever he sees the flash of a fish, but he never tries to catch one. He knows that goldfish are only happy when they are swimming in the water.

Other times, we climb into the branches of the friendly oak tree and watch the cotton wool clouds scudding by.

Charlie flicks his ears whenever a cloud goes by, but he never tries to reach out and catch one. He knows that clouds are too far away to touch.

And sometimes, we peek through the holes in the scratchy hedge next to the road and watch the busy people hurrying by.

Charlie wrinkles his nose whenever someone hurries past, but he never tries to go with them. He knows we have each other and that's enough.

Best of all, we like to chase the beautiful butterflies fluttering in the garden.

Charlie likes to run and jump when he sees their fluttering wings, but he never really catches them. He knows that butterflies are too beautiful to hurt.

Then one day, when Charlie and I were sitting in the grass by the little pond, Mum and Dad came to talk to me.
They told me that we were going to move house.

We were going to live in a great big flat in the city, with a lift and a playroom just for me and my toys.

'And will the garden have a pond and a friendly oak tree for Charlie?' I asked.

That's when Mum told me that we wouldn't have a garden.

'But Charlie loves the garden,' I said. 'We don't need a lift, or a playroom for me and my toys, but we do need a garden for Charlie. He will be very sad if he can't go outside.'

Mum and Dad agreed. That's why they thought it would be better to let Charlie stay with my cousins. They have a big garden with a pond and butterflies and two cats who could make friends with him.

'But I'm Charlie's best friend,' I said, 'he doesn't need any other friends.'

'But if Charlie was very sad, you would be very sad too,' my mum said. 'Friends always want each other to be happy.'

I stroked Charlie's soft black fur sadly. He put his head on my lap and looked up at me with his huge green eyes, and I knew my mum was right.

I couldn't let him be unhappy.

The day we left Charlie at my cousins' it felt like there was a great big hole inside me.

When I said goodbye to him, he wouldn't look at me and he kept his whiskers very still.

It's always hard for friends to say goodbye, especially best friends.

Our new flat is amazing and I love living in the city. We don't need a garden, because we have a park with a playground and a big, grassy field in it. It even has a duck pond and a pool that we can paddle in when the sun is shining.

I have lots of new friends and whenever we can, we play together. It's fun having so many people to play with and we always think of different things to do.

Sometimes we swing so high
in the playground that we
almost reach the cotton wool
clouds as they scud by. Then I
have to smile, because Charlie
and I know that clouds are too
far away to touch.

Other times, we dip our toes in the sparkly water of the paddling pool and shiver because it is so cold, then I wonder if the water in the pond in Charlie's garden is cold enough to make him flick his ears.

And sometimes we play hide-and-seek under the branches of the weepy trees that grow by the pond.

When I peek through the wispy leaves and watch my friends looking for me, I laugh to think how much looking at them would make Charlie wrinkle his nose.

Best of all, my friends and I like to chase each other around the big, grassy field. While we're running around, I think of Charlie playing with his new cat friends and I feel very happy.

Making new friends is always exciting.

I visit Charlie as often as I can. When I run through the door of my cousins' house he looks at me with his huge green eyes, wiggles his long whiskers and purrs loudly.

We are even happier to see each other now.

Charlie really likes his new home. He still loves the garden and plays in it all the time with his new cat friends.

But even though the pond has sparkly goldfish and the garden has a friendly oak tree, they never sit together to watch the flashing fish or the scudding clouds.

And when Charlie is with them, he doesn't seem to notice the busy people hurrying by on the other side of the scratchy hedge, he doesn't even like to run and jump when the beautiful butterflies flutter by.

He waits for me to do
all those things.
   We both know that
some things are so special
you can only do them
with your best friend.